# This Winnie-the-Pooh book belongs to

..................................................

# Farshore

First published in Great Britain 2021 by Farshore
An imprint of HarperCollins*Publishers*
1 London Bridge Street, London SE1 9GF
www.farshore.co.uk

HarperCollins*Publishers*
1st Floor, Watermarque Building, Ringsend Road
Dublin 4, Ireland

Written by Jude Exley
Designed by Pritty Ramjee
Illustrated by Eleanor Taylor and Mikki Butterley

Copyright © 2021 Disney Enterprises, Inc.
Based on the "Winnie the Pooh" works
by A.A.Milne and E.H.Shepard

ISBN 978 0 7555 0122 9

Printed in Italy
001

# Winnie-the-Pooh

## A Present from Pooh

**Farshore**

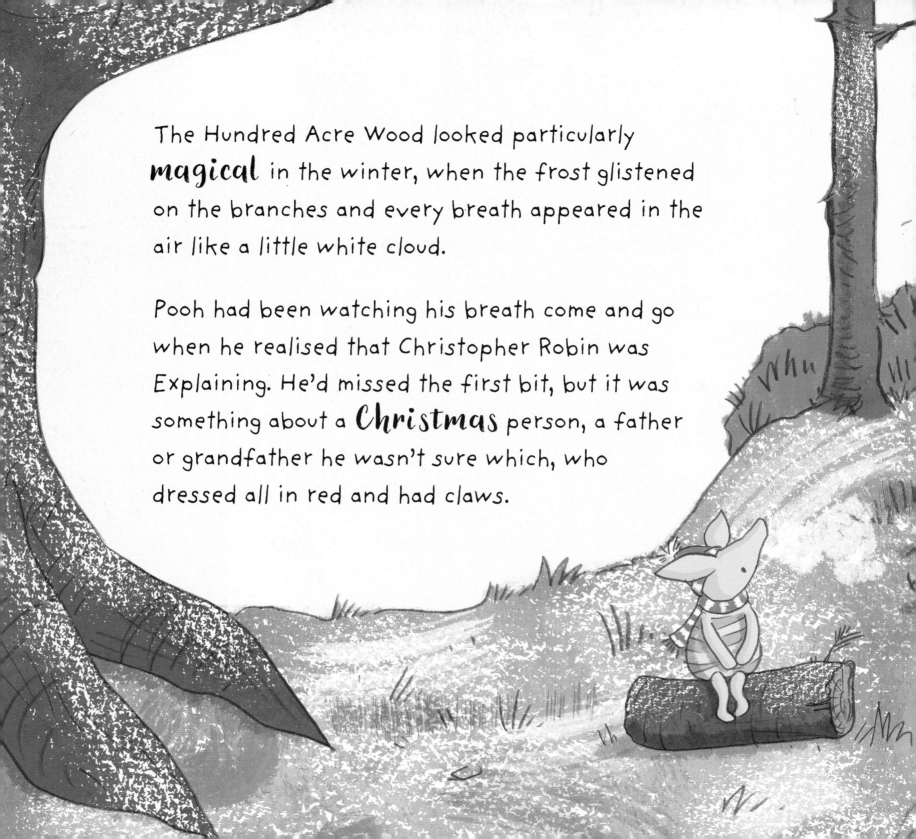

The Hundred Acre Wood looked particularly **magical** in the winter, when the frost glistened on the branches and every breath appeared in the air like a little white cloud.

Pooh had been watching his breath come and go when he realised that Christopher Robin was Explaining. He'd missed the first bit, but it was something about a **Christmas** person, a father or grandfather he wasn't sure which, who dressed all in red and had claws.

"Claws?" asked Piglet anxiously.

"Not the sharp ones," explained Christopher Robin.
"He's **kind** and gives presents."

"**Presents!**" squealed Roo. "I like those."

"Perhaps we could be this Christmassy Father Santa
Claws person for each other, as a surprise,"
suggested Pooh.

"I'm not sure I like **surprises**," said Eeyore gloomily. "Not after Tigger bounced me into the river."

"This will be a **fun** surprise, Eeyore," said Christopher Robin, kindly. "We'll all give someone a **present.**"

"I did get a Useful Pot and a burst balloon for my birthday once," said Eeyore.

"You did indeed," said Pooh proudly.

And so it was decided that Owl would write down their names on pieces of paper and they would each pick a name out of Christopher Robin's woolly hat.

Some of the friends picked their own name at first or needed help with reading, but soon all the friends had someone they would give a **gift** to.

Kanga and Roo were sharing, as mothers and children often do.

"I'm just glad that the big man with the claws isn't coming to visit me," said Pooh, who was still rather puzzled.

"Oh, Pooh," laughed Christopher Robin, "let's walk home together and I'll tell you all about **Father Christmas** and his magical visits."

The next day, Kanga and Roo began making their gift for Tigger.

"Biscuits!" cried Roo. "I hope Tigger will share them," but then he changed his mind. They were extract of malt biscuits. Tigger's **favourite**, but not Roo's!

"Roo dear, you can lick the spoon now," said Kanga, as she popped the biscuits in the oven to bake.

"**Yuck!**" giggled Roo.

Meanwhile, Tigger was **bouncing** in a thinking
kind of way, with his warm scarf **flapping** around
him. The thinking was about what to give Eeyore.

Perhaps a floating balloon like the one Eeyore
should have got, but didn't? But balloons were more
for sunshiny days than for frosty days ...

Just then, a **gust** of icy wind gave
Tigger a Kind and Generous idea ...

Little did Eeyore know that Tigger had such a generous gift in mind as he gathered **haycorns** for Piglet.

"Brr, my nose is getting colder with each haycorn I find," he grumbled as he pushed them together.

But really, Eeyore was **pleased** that he was doing this for Piglet and he had known exactly what to give him and just which pot to put the haycorns in.

Piglet was warm and cosy indoors baking a **honey** cake for Pooh. As he poured in the sticky, sweet honey, he could imagine Pooh **licking** every last crumb from his paws.

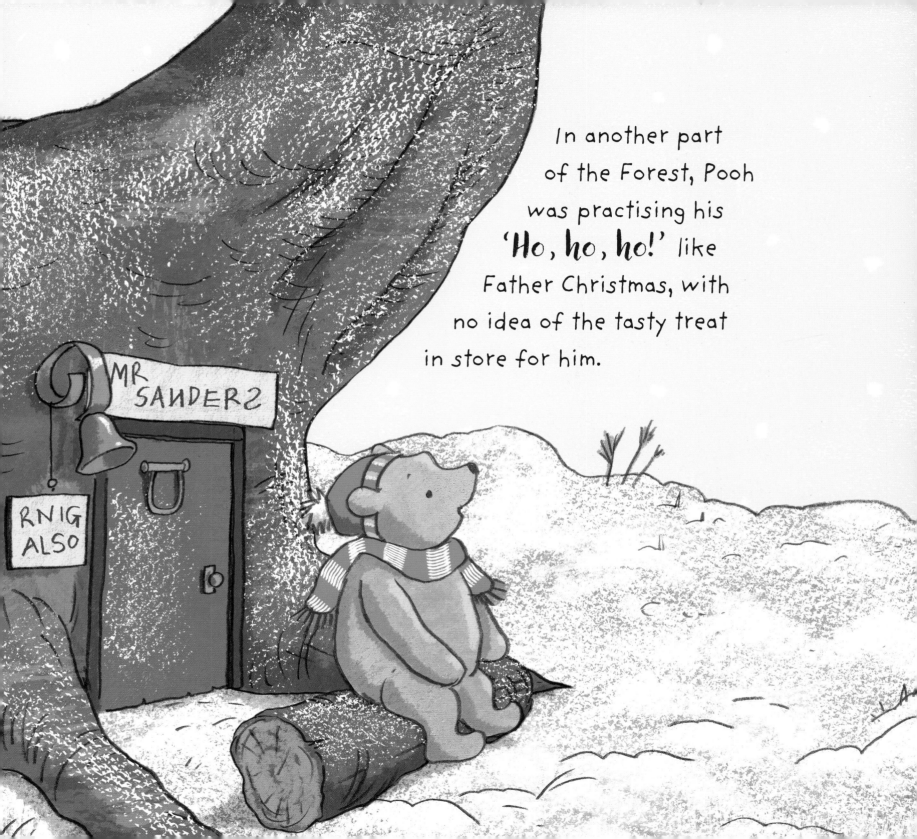

In another part
of the Forest, Pooh
was practising his
'Ho, ho, ho!' like
Father Christmas, with
no idea of the tasty treat
in store for him.

Owl was much more serious as he wrote '**WHerE PooH GoT STuK**' on a sign for Rabbit to hang beside his door. Such a memorable event needed a special sign.

While Rabbit was surrounded by things he'd **collected** from the Forest, as he made a wind chime for Kanga and Roo to listen to in the breeze.

"Is everyone present for the presents?" began Rabbit on the day of the gift giving, which was rather confusing,

but all the **friends** were there

and after a flurry of paper and ribbons,

there were just two **presents** left to be opened.

"**Thank you** for my new pencils, Christopher Robin," said Owl, proudly. "Now you must open your present."

With that, Christopher Robin
bent down and picked up a
rolled up piece of
paper with his
name on it.

It was a hum from Pooh, which Christopher Robin sang
to them all:

Ho, ho, ho, it's Christmas time,
Ho, ho, ho and here's my rhyme,
It's a song of good cheer,
For a friend who is dear -
The gift that lasts all year!

And so the day ended with a poem about friends and sharing gifts and the cold winter air didn't feel quite as cold in the warm glow of their friendship.

# Enjoy other wintery tales with Winnie-the-Pooh and friends!

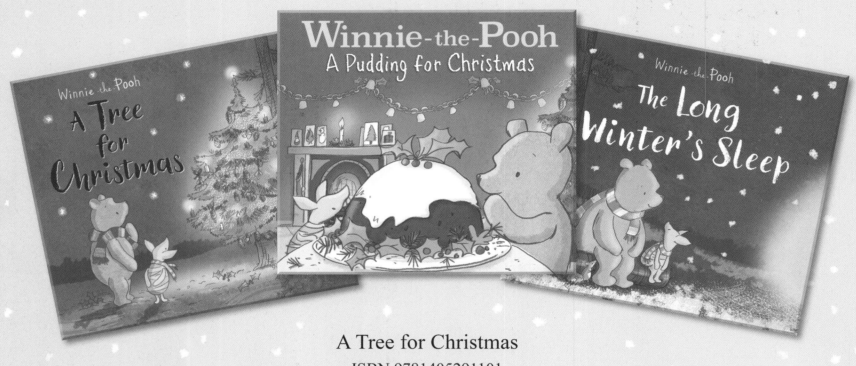

A Tree for Christmas
ISBN 9781405291101

A Pudding for Christmas
ISBN 9781405297875

The Long Winter's Sleep
ISBN 9781405294591